EAVESDROPPING

FRIENDS AND ENCOUNTERS

BY KAMYRA HARDING

Thank you for picking up the third installment of Eavesdropping. With this book, I've fulfilled my promise to collate the conversations I used to share on Facebook. Although many are new, I hope you'll recognize your favorites. Thank you for encouraging me to publish these books. This third and final book in the Eavesdropping series is the most illustrative of what happens when we interact with people who aren't different from us. The outcome can be educational or scary, but mostly, it's beautiful. Now that I've caught up, look out for new eavesdropping social media posts. There's always good stuff to overhear.

Table of Contents

Introduction

It's amazing what you overhear when you're open to eavesdropping on other people's business. When she was a child, Kamyra and her father would pick out strangers in a setting and make up conversations and backgrounds to fit the scene before them.

Kamyra upholds this practice as an adult, even if her sons only do it occasionally to humor her. This book contains conversations she's overheard, participated in, or imagined. They are the perfect length for when you don't have time to get lost in a novel. These scenes are ideal for actors to use to sharpen their skills. Rumor has it Kamyra has used a few as dream seed planters. Dream seed planters are when you continue one of the conversations in your mind as you settle yourself for sleep. If successful, the scene you're conjuring will manifest into a full-fledged dream. It's a great way to keep the monsters at bay.

GIRL TALK

Scene: Two women sitting on a park bench.

Lucy:
I don't understand why you are against President Trump.
You're a New Yorker. You were there during 911. Don't
you want us to protect the country so terrorists and drug
dealers can't get in? Shouldn't we spend our money
fortifying this country instead of donating to countries
that created their own problems?

Nadine:
I'm against calling entire groups of people murderers,
rapists, thugs, and terrorists. I'm against reducing public
thought to hateful stereotypes. I'm against being an
inhospitable nation.

I was in the thick of it during 911. I've lived the horror of a
terrorist attack. More than fearing another one, I fear
living in the type of country that produces terrorists, a
country whose leaders label groups as unworthy
because of their religion, race, or ethnicity. I fear living in
a country where my children can't walk down the street
without being harassed by people the president has
sanctioned to rain evil down upon the land.

Lucy:
You're exaggerating. People don't do that. I haven't
heard of anything like that. And we have laws to protect
your children.

Nadine:
People have been doing that and are doing it even
more lately. My nephew was followed. A niece was

verbally abused at school. It's not happening to your children because they look like the attackers. You haven't heard about these incidents because you choose to ignore and dismiss accounts like you just did to mine. When my kids leave the house, I don't fear they will be caught in a terrorist attack. I fear that one of the many racists emboldened by the president will harm them. I fear that White supremacist police officers will kill them.

Lucy:
Humph. What about the police being killed?

Nadine:
I want to live in a country where neither parents nor law enforcement families have to worry every time their loved ones walk out of the door. I don't want to live in a country where one side hates the other so much that they attack them physically and institutionally. I don't want to live in a country where people are so tired of being fearful that they rise up in violence. I want to live in a country that is safe for all.

Lucy:
That sounds pretty, but it isn't realistic. We need to put an end to all of this.

Nadine:
All of what?

Lucy:
Huh? Things aren't the same.

Nadine:
True. Unlike in the recent and distant past, we were edging our way toward equity. Because that means those with advantages may have to sacrifice a bit to help others, those with advantages flew into a rage. The president represents that rage. The problem is that, unlike the president, rage doesn't discriminate. I want to live in a country free of rage. That's why I do the work that I do. This isn't theoretical for me.

Lucy:
You don't get it. We must be safe. He doesn't really mean all Mexicans are rapists or all Muslims are terrorists. But until we can tell which are, we have to keep them all out.

Nadine:
Then why did he say it?

Lucy:
Say what?

Nadine:
If he doesn't believe all Mexicans are rapists, why did he say it? I can't read hearts and minds. I have to believe what people say. I'm forced to believe he means it when he spews ugliness.

Lucy:
Fine. But his uncouthness is a small price to pay to get the country back on track. I don't care for him as a man, but we need him to regain our place in the world.

Nadine:
If you support a hater, you are a hater by proximity.

Lucy:
If it's so bad, maybe you should just move.

Nadine:
This is my home just as much as it is his or yours. I don't have to leave because it's not perfect. I will stay. Cast light on hate and work to end it. Abandoning the hard work isn't an option.

Lucy:
You don't get it.

Nadine:
True. I don't understand hate.

REAL TALK
Scene: Two men in a baby nursery

Tony:
Man! I didn't know assembling baby stuff was this
complicated. I need another beer.

Kevin:
Tell me about it. We'd better figure this out before Asha
comes in here and 'does it her damn self.'

Tony:
I know that's right. Your woman don't play. Pass me the
socket wrench. I think I figured out this part. Would help if
y'all bought some American products with instructions in
English.

Kevin:
I've got your English. Keep working.

Tony:
Real talk, Kev; what's it like knowing you'll be a father in
a few months?

Kevin:
It's exciting and intimidating all at the same time. I feel
like The Man because I knocked up my wife. I'm
embarrassingly sentimental over meeting the baby.
Want to see if it looks like me or her; all that crap. But I'm
scared. This is serious business. When I proposed to Asha,
I knew she was the only woman for me. But in the back
of my mind, I knew that if I was wrong, we could get
divorced. Not that I was planning on it. She's my heart.

But if there was a problem, I knew the solution. I can't divorce a kid. A kid needs me to be on point, always. Gotta provide, protect, and answer endless questions. What if I get something wrong? I could screw up a little person.

Tony:
That's deep.

Kevin:
Don't get me wrong. I'm more excited than anything, but I do wonder. The best part is that Asha will be the perfect mother. She already is. Hell, she calms me down when I get nervous about the whole deal. It's like she already has it figured out.

Tony:
Guess that means you can never divorce her. It's about more than you two now.

Kevin:
Yeh. What about you? When will we be assembling things for your kid?

Tony:
I'm not trying to have any baby mamas.

Kevin:
What about a wife? You can't keep sampling the honey.

Tony:
It's not about that. At least it hasn't been for a while. If I met the future Mrs. Douglas, I'd fall into step: marriage,

house, kids, gas-guzzling ride, Disney vacations, and all. I can get with that program.

Kevin:
What about Cindy? Seemed like you two were headed in that direction. What was wrong with her?

Tony:
Nothing. Apparently, I wasn't forever for her.

Kevin:
That's what happened? Later for her. Don't stress it. Mrs. Douglas is out there. Have fun until you find her.

Tony:
Actually, while we're on the subject, I think there is someone.

Kevin:
Who?

Tony:
You know her. She's been here all along.

Kevin:
(Considering possibilities. The least likely person pops into his mind)

Ah. Don't go there.

Tony:
Afraid I have to.

Kevin:
Nah, bruh. Pat?

Tony:
The one and only?

Kevin:
She's like a sister to us. We all grew up together. Isn't there anyone else? Pat? Since when?

Tony:
Not sure when it began, but I'm tired of denying it. Planning on talking to her later today. Asking her on a real date, the whole thing.

Kevin:
This makes my head hurt.

Tony:
She does it for me. I think I do it for her—time to find out.

Kevin:
Fine. If you mess up, I'll have to kick your ass.

Tony:
I'm not trying to mess up. I wouldn't make this move if I weren't serious.

Kevin:
Ring set serious?

Tony:
Probably should have a first date before claiming that but yes.

Kevin:
Hold up; this could be good. If you guys get together, you can babysit for us. Practice handling a baby. It's difficult, but we'd sacrifice for your education.

Tony:
Selfish prick, I'd rather practice making a baby with her.

Kevin:
TMI! I can't unhear that!

EXCLUSIVE INCLUSION
Scene: Neighbors talking in their driveways.

Bryson:

Have you found a pediatrician? I'm having a hard time finding a Black one in our area.

Liliana:

We found one a while ago. You'll only go with African Americans? Why?

Bryson:

We want our kids to know they can be anything they want to be. One way to do that is to expose them to people who look like them and who are doing all kinds of things.

Liliana:

(Skeptically)

Really?

Bryson:

Our parents did it for us.

Liliana:

(Sarcastically)

And it worked? That's why you do your job?

Bryson:

(Laughing)

Using that logic, they failed.

(Seriously)

It worked because I never saw limits. I didn't become a pediatrician, but I knew I could.

Liliana:
I still don't get it. Why does your pediatrician have to be Black? Ours is White. He's fantastic. You're segregating yourselves.

Bryson:
Why is choosing to spend my money on Black professionals an issue for you?

Liliana:
Wasn't the Civil Rights Movement about African Americans being able to go to White doctors and such?

Bryson:
My understanding of The Movement is that, like the Women's Rights Movement, it was about freedom of choice. I choose these people. I am not forced to patronize them.

Liliana:
I think you're putting lipstick on a pig.

Bryson:
What's the race, ethnic and religious background of your dentist? Accountant? Lawyer?

Liliana:
That's different.

Bryson:
Why?

Liliana:
There are more qualified White professionals.

Bryson:
Not according to my contact list. I'm happy to give you non-White, Christian, male referrals.

WHAT'S IN A NAME?

Scene: Ladies' room sink during halftime of a junior high school basketball game.

BBall Mom 1:
What's your name again?

BBall Mom 2:
Kamyra

BBall Mom 1:
What do people call you?

BBall Mom 2:
Kamyra

BBall Mom 1:
I'm going to call you Kay.

BBall Mom 2:
OK, but I may not know who you are talking to.

HOVERBOARD PROFESSIONALS

Scene: After an intense conversation about Hoverboard fires, who purchased and returned Hoverboards this past holiday season, three women who had just met in the swimming pool concluded their talk with:

Katy (From Atlanta):
I'm a nurse, and the first thing I thought when I saw one was elbow fractures and such.

Scout (From Toronto):
I'm a lawyer, so…

Andrea (From Manhattan):
See. I'm an educator, so I thought, "They'll learn."

SHUTTING IT DOWN

Breanna:
You're not really Black.

Logan:
Well, I'm president of the Black students' group, so I must be.

(Mic Drop!)

THE INTERVENTION

Scene: Three fashionable, professional women
in their 30s, drinking wine in a modern living
room decorated in leather, chrome, slate, and glass.

Whitley:

Teresa and I want to talk to you about your
engagement. We think you're being swayed by good
sex and haven't thought about your future. Don't get me
wrong. Carter is nice and all. But are you sure he's
marriage material?

Teresa:

You know we love you. We three are a team for life.
That's why we have to say something.

Gwen:

(Sarcastically)

Ooh goodie! Are we playing that game where we each
tell the others about themselves? If so, I have a list for the
two of you.

Teresa:

This is serious, honey. We have real concerns about
Carter.

Gwen:

I understand. I have real concerns about your choices. If
you're 'bout to get into my business, it's fair that I get
equal time in yours. I thought we had the type of
friendship where we respect one another and our
choices. That's why I've always supported both of you.

Apparently, I was wrong. Go ahead. Save me from myself, and I'll return the favor.

Whitley:
Don't get defensive. We're not hating. We think you could do better. That's all.

Teresa:
You're amazing. Any man would be lucky to have you. We're not sure Carter understands you.

Gwen:
Why not? He speaks English.

Teresa:
Yes. But you're different types of people.

Gwen:
How so?

Teresa:
Well -

Whitley:
What she means is that he brings less to the table than you. He doesn't have a degree. You have three. He's blue-collar. You travel on a private corporate jet. He's out of place in your world.

Gwen:
Is that what you thought when you were hanging with your trainer?

Whitley:
He was a plaything. That relationship wasn't meant to go anywhere.

Gwen:
Please stop. You're embarrassing yourselves. You're supposed to be progressive feminists. Since when does one of our men have to earn more? Why can't he work with his hands? Your fathers did.

Whitley:
Our fathers didn't have a choice. Our children's fathers don't have to be laborers. Be realistic. He doesn't fit into your world. Clients and co-workers will stop taking you seriously when they meet him.

Gwen:
Enough. He's a great guy. He goes to work every day without complaint. He loves me completely and makes my life easier by contributing in ways that money can't buy. And the sex isn't good. It's great.

Teresa:
I understand the attraction. But how long can it last? Eventually, you'll need a peer.

Gwen:
Like your husband? The one that threw you a lavish 30th birthday party one month, then took his mistress on vacation the next?

Teresa:
Wha-

Whitley:
Save it. This isn't about her.

Gwen:
That's right. This is about me receiving your unsolicited advice. How about this? I'd rather receive bath salts for my birthday from a faithful man than an emerald ring from a cheater.

Teresa:
No one is suggesting you accept a man that cheats. We're looking out for you. We wouldn't be here if we didn't care. We love you. You can do so much better than settling.

Gwen:
Thank you for your concern. Listen closely; I'm saying this only once. Carter is a good man. I'm lucky to have him. We are life peers. We talk about books, listen to the same music, and we're training together for a road race. I trust him. Thus far, my clients adore him. Well, except when he's beating them on the golf course. Yes. He golfs. He also bowls and plays poker. Since we've been together, I haven't had to call a repair person, mechanic, or for takeout. I don't want his money. That's the point of making my own. What I need, he provides. He listens. He's supportive. He helps me be a better person. I spend less time at the office these days, yet I am more productive. The migraines are gone, and I sleep through the night.

Whitley:
OK, OK. We're not going to get anywhere today. Just know that we'll be here when it doesn't work out.

Gwen:

Really? I suppose I should say, "Thanks." What I really want is my turn to judge you. Are we there yet? No? Then I'll be the supportive friend and discard my prejudices.

(Raises wine glass)

To my engagement.

BAMBOOZLED

Scene: Parents sitting on a park bench
watching their children on the playground.

Carter:
Soooo remember all the trouble my kid was having with
Pedro a few years ago? Well, come to find out, my kid
started most of that crap. He thought it was funny.

Indira:
What do you mean?

Carter:
Last night we were watching a movie where kids were
goading a boy until he exploded. He cracked up,
saying how they used to do that to Pedro. I was so
angry. I told him/her to apologize. You know I went to
bat for him/her. Remember? I even emailed and spoke
to Pedro's parents about his anger issues. I feel so stupid.

Salma:
It's OK. You didn't know. You trusted your kid. We have
to.

Carter:
Oh well, my kid is probably right. That was a long time
ago. Can you believe it? Frickin' amazing.

Salma:
Don't be too hard on him/her. Kids make mistakes. Let it
go. Pedro is fine. He has friends and gets good grades.
It's no big deal.

Carter:
You're right. I was being dramatic.

Indira:
I don't know. I have been in Pedro's parents' shoes. It's never too late. An acknowledgment, if not a full-on apology, would go a long way.

PERSPECTIVE

Scene: Co-workers seated in a conference
room speaking before a meeting

Incensed:
I don't need Madison Avenue to tell me when to
celebrate someone. I can communicate my love on my
own. I can give a gift just because.

Mellow:
True. Everyone says that, but few do it. I understand the
economics behind greeting card holidays. How much to
spend on whom is my decision. In theory, I can
celebrate people any day of the year. In practice, not
so much. I don't mind a reminder to stop and
acknowledge someone.

Incensed:
You have a point. I'm always too busy to do the nice
things I want to do for others. Guess a holiday reminder is
nice. It encourages you to stop and do.

Mellow:
Yep. No one's forcing you.

Incensed:
In a way, they are forcing you. There's cultural pressure
to participate.

Mellow:
You don't have to bow to the pressure. Do what you
want, how you want. It's not a struggle if you're being
authentic. You have to own the pressure for it to work.

Incensed:
Easier said than done. People have expectations.

Mellow:
What you're talking about has less to do with holidays and more to do with perspective. The change needs to be within you, not the rest of the world.

MINDING YOUR BUSINESS

Scene: White, Jewish male and African
American female acquaintances talking in his
shop. A third customer, unknown to the female friend,
leans into their conversation.

Customer:
Atlanta! Why would you move there? That place is
awful! I was on assignment there for a month; me a
Jewish woman. It was horrendous! Those people...

What could you possibly be looking forward to there?

Female Acquaintance:
My son not being the only Black child in his circles.

Customer:
Oh.

(Glances down at goods for purchase)

WHAT'S YOUR BUSY?

Scene: Discussing a mutual friend's hard times.

Melba:

She needs help. Soraia, you have nothing better to do. Why don't you help her?

(Melba walks away in a commanding Mistress of the Universe manner)

Clara:

Can you believe her? Why didn't you set her straight? I know you're plenty busy with a job, seriously sick parents, a traveling husband, and everything else you do. And unlike some people, you don't have a nanny. Does she know you lost two family members this year? You need to tell people what's up.

Soraia:

It's OK. She's (b)itchy because she's unhappy. I like my job and love my family. My busy is good. Hers is a burden.

CLOTHING BUSINESS
Scene: Mothers at a cocktail party

Nguyet:
These girls are dressing too skanky for this.

Maissa:
They don't know how to be appropriate. Mine notices
and talks about the others.

Nguyet:
They need to be taught right from wrong. I put it this way
to mine. You wouldn't wear a snowsuit in the hot tub.
Would you?

Marissa:
Yes. Clothes for each occasion. Club clothes do not
belong at work.

Karma:
I tell mine to mind their business. They don't like to be
told what to wear, so don't tell others.

CAUSE & EFFECT

Scene: Conversation between college freshmen. One is the child of Greek immigrants—the other is a first-generation Afro-Latina-Caribbean American.

G:

I'm sorry, ALC, but at my high school, the smart kids took French, and the others took Spanish. It's just the way things are.

ALC:
(Internal dialogue)

I'm here to learn. I don't want to spend four years correcting statements like that.

(External response)

That's ignorant.

Note:
After numerous more microaggressions G questioned why ALC "segregated" herself with other students from the African diaspora.

CELL SERVICE

Scene: A seasoned diva speaking with a service representative as she prepares to transition from a flip to a smartphone.

Service Rep:
... then go to the App Store--

Diva:
Where is that? How do I get there from here?

UNSOLICITED, INCORRECT, USELESS ADVICE

Scene: Red just explained to Blue, a zealous pet owner, why she doesn't have furry family members. Red liken her feelings to the pressure child-free couples feel at Thanksgiving dinner when well-meaning, nosy family and friends insist that they must raise kids.

Blue:
You should get one of those hypoallergenic dogs or a hairless cat.

Red:
Can't. I'm highly allergic to pet dander.

Blue:
But those aren't as bad. It's just one animal. The Obamas have…

Red:
What you said is analogous to telling someone with a peanut allergy to schemer creamy peanut butter instead of chunky on their toast.

COLLATERAL DAMAGE

Scene: College coeds eating pizza in a dorm room.

Yusef:
How was the funeral?

Zora:
Peachy. Nothing like being an outsider within your own family. Once upon a time, I was in like Flynn. Now I'm the kid from her first marriage. The one everyone wants to pretend didn't happen.

Yusef:
That bad?

Zora:
They didn't have a place for me at the head table. It was as if I was a guest.

Yusef:
I feel you. I'm a reminder of a past my parents would like to erase. Both have new and improved families. My stepmother pretends my father wasn't married before.

Zora:
Mine sent holiday cards with them in one shot and me in an extra little square on the side.

Yusef:
My stepfather is cool. He treats me like the other kids. But sometimes, when I'm introduced to his friends, I realize they didn't know I existed. I'm a dirty little secret.

Dolly:
It's different for me because I was raised in the house with my stepdad. He did carpool and stuff. We were one big messy family.

Zora:
Lucky you.

Dolly:
It wasn't a fairytale. I was constantly navigating having a relationship with him and giving my bio dad his respect. Each expected some kind of unknown allegiance from me. For the most part, we're cool now. They're even cool with each other. In the beginning, they were faking it. Eventually, they reached an unspoken understanding. Maybe it was spoken. They were men enough to do it without my knowledge. Whatever. At least I have both of them. I can totally see both walking me down the aisle, like in that video that went viral last year.

Yusef:
I wish.

Zora:
Your parents should teach a course.

COVER-UPS
Scene: Office break room

Jerry:
I feel you. I'm followed all the time in stores. They see the tats and assume I'm up to no good. It's offensive. Sometimes I just can't deal.

Orlando:
What happens when you can't deal?

Jerry:
I wear long pants and sleeves. No one messes with me when I'm covered.

Orlando:
When I don't want to deal, I can't go out. I can't hide my race and stuff. If I'm out, it happens. Can't deal. Stay home.

TRENDY HAPPINESS
Scene: Office copy room

Fiona:
Cute blouse. Is it a Trendy Boo Boo?

Pink:
Thanks. Girl, I got this from Discount Hut.

Fiona:

(Recoiling)

Really?

Pink:
Yes. If I had the money, I could buy the designer version. I'd be more stylish. But I wouldn't be happier. This shirt makes me smile. Would I smile brighter if it cost more?

REAL MEN

Scene: Grocery store checkout line

Irvin:

What's that in your cart? Man! I'd never be caught with female products. What kind of man are you?

Birch:

Is that right? Let's compare carts. Mine says I have a woman. Yours says...

STRAIGHT 2 THE TOP

Scene: Jane Q Public is on the phone with a service provider insisting upon a service the company does not offer.

Jane Q Public:
Let me speak with the supervisor.

Staffer:
I am the supervisor.

Jane Q Public:
Then get me your boss.

Staffer:
I am the boss.

VIVA LA DIFFERENCE

Scene: Mothers on the sideline of a soccer field

Bobbi:
Norm is at every game, and he volunteers on campus.
What does he do?

Sabrina:
He's a soccer dad.

Mateo:
No. He works out of his house. He has an office and gets
paid.

Sabrina:
So do I, but you call me a soccer mom. What's the
difference?

FOR THE GAZILLIONTH TIME
Scene: Co-workers having lunch in a park

Becky:
I stopped reading your posts because you hate White women.

Khadija:
No. I call out myopic and hypocritical views of feminism.

Becky:
Well, your posts aren't diverse. It's all Black people this and Black people that.

Khadija:
I'm Black. Pictures of my friends and family will have a lot of Black people in them. I care about issues that affect the people I love. But if you scroll down my page, you'll see posts about all kinds of things.

Becky:
I just think you shouldn't post so much about race. It's divisive.

Khadija:
I wish there wasn't a need to post that stuff. I also wish people would let everyone be themselves. I'm fed up with the idea that non-White, non-straight, non-Cristian people must change so that White, straight, CIS Christians can be comfortable.

Becky:
Why should we be made to feel bad? We can't help what we are. Why bombard people with all of that race stuff? We need less of that and more positivity.

Khadija:
If me posting inoffensive stuff about Black & Brown people on my personal page makes you feel bad, that's your issue. I don't have to change my essence for your comfort. That would make me uncomfortable in my own space.

Becky:
Surely you agree that you can compromise? That's what people do in polite society.

Khadija:
Then you change. Aren't you a member of polite society?

MORNING CONNECTION

Scene: Breakfast bistro line.

The barista confuses orders. People receive incorrect drinks, wait too long, and suffer from coffee deprivation. When the flustered barista retreats to the kitchen to assess the situation, Customer 1 and Customer 3 bond over complaining about the low-quality service.

Barista:
Good Morning. May I help you?

Customer 2:
Yes, you may. First, take a moment and breathe.

Barista:
(Looks up shocked. Makes meaningful eye contact with Customer 2 exhales and smiles)

Customer 2:
Better?

PERFECTION IS NOT REQUIRED
Scene: Coffee shop counter

Cashier:
Hello. How are you today?

Customer:
Fine. Thanks. How are you?

Cashier:
Fan... Well... I'm fantastic. Yeh. I'm fantastic.

Customer:
That should be the definition of fantastic. Not the absence of problems. Fantastic isn't perfection. It's smiling and happiness despite problems.

Cashier:
(smiling)

You've got something there. Call Webster's!

ALLEGIANCE

Scene: Neighbors catching up across cars
parked in adjacent driveways

Alastair:

Democrats need to have a seat. They lost. Get over it.
Pursuing legal charges against President Trump would
be bad for the country. We have to move on from the
election. Despite his illegal actions, Republicans didn't
impeach President Obama.

Lenwood:

Not for a lack of trying. Which proven illegalities? They
couldn't find anything on President Obama. Do you
really think he'd have lasted a day beyond the
discovery of anything illegal? If there was anything
prosecutable, it would have been used, and not just by
Republicans. Plenty of Democrats would have sacrificed
the party and prosecuted him. Racism trumps patriotism.

LOST IN TRANSLATION

Scene: Woman ordering dinner in a popular restaurant.

Diner:
I'll have the wild mushroom st-roz-za-pre-ti. Is that how you pronounce it?

Waitress:
I say pasta.

TAKING CARE OF BUSINESS

Scene: Two men of different generations touring an empty house.

Gil:

This is the best I can do for now. It's not impressive, but I can maintain it if the team cuts me. Don't want to go so big that I have to sell it out from under you if I lose the gig. When I'm more flush, we'll upgrade you.

Thompson:

You don't have to do this?

Gil:

I know. Except I do. You're the reason I'm here. Not just the reason I play but why I am alive. You saved my life.

Thompson:

It was my job.

Gil:

Your job was to maintain a file. Not to take me from a homeless case number to All American.

Thompson:

One and the same.

Gil:

Hardly. Anyway, I'm not the only one you saved, but for now, I'm the only one who can put this kind of roof over your head.

Thompson:
I have a home.

Gil:
Rent it out. Sell it. I don't care. Now you have a nicer one
to live in.

Thompson:
I know you aren't telling me what to do.

Gil:
No, sir. Please do it for me. Knowing you're safe makes it
easier for me to be so far away. That and knowing a few
of the other guys are here with you. We got you just like
you had us, Coach.

PRIORITIES

Scene: After the app shows that no ride shares are available in the area, Carey calls Joe for a quick pickup from an after-hours party in a desolate area.

Joe:
Hello.

Carey:
Yo. Man.

Joe:
Whasup?

(Woman's seductive voice in background)

Can't talk. Gotta go. Catch you tomorrow.

Carey:
Wait.

(Joe has already hung up, lured by distracting sweet promises.)

(Carey is mugged while dialing Joe again.)

EVERYTHING CHANGES

Scene: A telephone conversation between two long-time, close friends. Laura is upset because Fran has a new friend.

Fran:
So, Tanya and I were at Uno's after work the other day.

Laura:
You've been hanging with Tanya a lot lately.

Fran:
I guess so. Anyway, we were talking about going on that Divine Nine cruise.

Laura:
Really? I thought we decided not to do that. Remember, I have Charles' family reunion that weekend.

Fran:
That's cool. I'll share a cabin with Tanya.

Laura:
So, what? Tanya's replaced me? You're spending a lot of time with her. I hardly see you these days.

Fran:
That's because you're married now. I can't wait around for you to have time for me. I don't complain about Charles being your priority. I get it. Being married alters your life. But you can't put a placeholder in me. You

marry, and life changes for everyone, not just you. Facts. We're still friends.

Laura:
Oh, so I'm out because I'm married.

Fran:
No. But my life doesn't stop because you're married. We're still friends. I love you. I have to adjust to you not hanging with me like you used to, and you have to get used to me doing things with other people. We're not joined at the hip anymore. Haven't been for a while. What did you think I was doing while you were on dates with Charles, taking romantic vacations, getting to know his family and stuff?

Laura:
I never really thought about it.

Fran:
Maybe you should have.

OFF LIMITS

Scene: Adolescent friends are walking from school to a subway station.

Cassandra:
I need to stop in the drugstore for my mother.

Trent:
OK, I'll go with you.

(Attractive, sophisticated looking same age youth approaches)

Harley:
Wassup, Trent? Whatch doin' out 'chere?

Trent:
Just comin from school.

Harley:
Who's the pretty lady?

Trent:
(Cursing under his breath)

Cassandra, meet Harley. Harley, Cassandra.

Cassandra:
Hi.

Harley:
Hi, Pretty. I like that bag.

Trent:
Go on in and get your mother's stuff. I'll wait out here.

Casandra:
Ummkay.

(Cassandra enters the store)

Trent:
Don't even think about it.

Harley:
What?

Trent:
Not only ain't she about that life, she don't know it exists.

Harley:
I'm offended.

Trent:
You got plenty. Leave her.

Harley:
Why? That you?

Trent:
Naw. Ain't me. But she's going to be somebody. Let her
be.

Harley:
It ain't all up to me.

Trent:
Come on, Man.

Harley:
Watch how you step to me, T. I see you in your feelings.
Imma give you this one.

Trent:
Appreciate it.

(Harley walks away just before Cassandra exits the store)

Cassandra:
What happened to Harley?

Trent:
He had to go.

Cassandra:
He's cute. He goes to your old school?

Trent:
Used to.

Cassandra:
He graduated?

Trent:
No. Harley's a dealer. You need to stay away from him. I
saw how you looked at him. Don't get any ideas. He's
dangerous. What happened to that corny dude you
were talking to?

Cassandra?
Come on. Harley is much cuter.

Trent:
I'm serious, Sandra. He's bad news.

Cassandra:
OK. Calm down. Corny Dude is all I can handle anyway.

(Walking in silence)

Trent

Trent:
What?

Cassandra:
Thank you.

Trent:
Whatever, Bighead.

PROTECTING YOU FROM ME

Scene: Teenage girl sees her grandfather on the street and tries to catch up with him when he enters an alley shortcut in route to their home. Three adolescent males are congregated in the alley. She doesn't notice one shaking his head at the others when she enters the alley.

Tory:
Oh, hi, Jason!

Jason:
(Faint smile)

Hey? Haven't seen you in a minute. School's good?

Tory:
Yep. How are things with you?

Jason:
No complaints. Just getting home?

Tory:
I was studying at the library. Finals are coming up.

Jason:
Good luck with that. Say "Hi" to the fam. Get home safe.

(Unbeknownst to Tory, acknowledging her family was code to others. She and hers are off limits, in every way, at all times.)

—Later that night, Tory overhears her grandparents sharing news of their days.—

Grandpa:
Saw Jason and a bunch of no-goods in the alley today.

Grandma:
Um. Doing what?

Grandpa:
Up to no good as usual.

Grandma:
How his mother cries over him; poor dear.

Grandpa:
She should.

(Silence)

Need to remind the kids not to take that shortcut.

JUDGY JUDGY

Scene: Two women sitting next to each in a high school auditorium.

Jan:
Hi. I'm Jan.

Cherlyn:
I'm Cherlyn.

Jan:
Do you have a student in the show?

Cherlyn:
My nephew plays Romeo.

Jan:
Oh, he's wonderful.

Cherlyn:
You've seen it already?

Jan:
This is my third time.

Cherlyn:
Why?

Jan:
My daughter is Juliet. I like to support her.

Cherlyn:
That's why I could never have children. I couldn't possibly attend every school performance like that. I have better things to do.

Jan:
This is my choice. If you had children, you could make a different choice. Your kids wouldn't expect you to attend every show if it's not you.

Cherlyn:
(Sheepishly)

I guess that's so.

DIVERSITY BEGINS WITH WHOM?
Scene: Childhood friends having brunch.

Madison:
Why is everyone in your Instagram pictures Black? You talk a lot about diversity. Shouldn't there be diversity in your life?

Althea:
My social media posts show my family. We're mostly Black. My life is diverse. I spend a lot of time in predominantly White professional and social situations. I post about that. Guess you missed those.

Madison:
You should have more. It's like you purposely exclude White people from your life. Shouldn't diversity begin with you if you're always talking about it?

Althea:
(Takes a deep breath)

Why am I the only Black person in your personal social pictures?

Madison:
You're the only one I really know. There aren't Black people like you in my neighborhood or other places I go.

Althea:
It's fine for you to avoid reaching out, but not me? Tell you what. Despite it not being my responsibility, I will

help you. I know plenty of Black, Brown, and Yellow people. You should spend more time hanging with me.

65

WHAT GOOD IS HE?

Scene: Four women enjoying happy hour at a
trendy lounge

Maxine:
My husband can't fix a thing. He'll replace anything
rather than figure out how to repair it.

Rebecca:
Mine too

Sabine:
Mine can figure out how to fix stuff, but he doesn't

Belle:
Mine can fix anything, but he's too busy working for
other people to work for me.

Maxine:
The only thing worse than my man paying repair people
is the blue-moon urges he gets to try fixing something.
He never picks a simple project. And always make the
problem worse. Then I'm like, "Let me call a
handyperson."

Rebecca:
Mine does that. I want to say, "Stay in your lane, honey."

Laughter

Maxine:
(Softly)

He does bring me tea

Belle:
Huh?

Maxine:
In the morning, he brings me a cup of tea.

Sabine:
Nice.

Rebecca:
Wait. He makes you tea every morning?

Maxine:
Yes. While his coffee is brewing.

Rebecca:
And he doesn't drink tea?

Maxine:
Nope.

(Silence)

Sabine:
(Wistfully)

That would be nice.

(Silence)

THE TRUTH

Scene: Friends watching a baseball game.

Cruz:
What are you looking for in a man?

Cara:
I'd like to find someone I trust enough to be vulnerable around.

Cruz:
You didn't have that with your ex.

Cara:
I thought we did, but he proved me wrong.

Cruz:
How? Ah. He cheated.

Cara:
Yes. But it was more than that

Cruz:
What?

Cara:
After the honeymoon period, he cheated, told my secrets to others, and was mean when I needed comfort.

Cruz:
How?

Cara:
He'd be mean whenever I cried about a death out of
fear or frustration.

Cruz:
Again, how?

Cara:
He'd lean into my face with a wicked look on his. Laugh
at me. Mock me. Tell me I had no right to cry. I never
understood it. I guess, in his eyes, I was supposed to be
flat. I could only express emotions that fed him? I don't
know.

Cruz:
Nah! Don't overanalyze it. Hard for you. I know. Sounds
as if he was sadistic. Hurt you for sport. Nothing more.

TO MOM, WITH LOVE

Scene: Lawyers catching up after Monday morning weekly status meeting. The supervising attorney has just reassigned to his protege a case that will necessitate him working through the weekend and long hours during the next week.

Calloway:
Let me know how I can help.

Johnson:
Sure thing, Boss. There is one thing you can do for me.

Calloway:
Name it.

Johnson:
Call my mother and explain to her that I won't be able to escort her on the family reunion cruise next week. The same cruise that's the first trip she's taken since my father died.

Calloway:
Johnson, it's not my job to make nice with your mommy. But if you need, I can hold your hand while you tell her.

Johnson:
Well, it's not my job to cancel three vacations in a row because you've lost your edge and won't go before the bench.

Calloway:
What'd you say?

Johnson:
Ahem. I'm not too proud to admit I'm scared of Mabel Johnson. If you want me here next week. You tell her. Remember when you met her? How'd that work out for you? I can't seem to remember. Hmmm? Why don't you remind me?

Calloway:
She chastised me with her eyes. Never said a word. Just cut straight through me. Wish I could do that. Would come in handy during depositions.

Johnson:
You don't say. Welcome to my childhood. Her number is
—

Calloway:
Fine. Go. Play with your mama. Make sure you pay for international Wi-Fi and roaming service. You're going to be on 24-hour consult.

Johnson:
Sure thing, Boss. I'll give Mabel your love.

GENEROSITY

Scene: Mom of a colicky newborn. Once she'd
gotten herself together enough to breathe, she
hand-delivered gifts to her condo neighbors as a thanks
for understanding and an apology for the noise.

New Mom:
Just a little something to say sorry for the crying at all
hours.

Retired Neighbor Man:
Nonsense, that's natural and beautiful. Enjoy him.

DRUMMER NEIGHBOR PLAYDATE

Scene 1: Woman exits an elevator in a luxury apartment building

Concierge:
How are you?

Athena:
Tired.

Concierge:
He kept you up last night?

Athena:
Yes. Hadn't begun that way. He was sleeping just fine.

Concierge:
What happened?

Athena:
Sometime after 2:00 am, the guy upstairs started playing the drums. Woke up 'lil man. Couldn't get him back to sleep. All he wanted to do was to play. We're all napping today.

Concierge:
Drums?

Athena:
I think he comes home jazzed after a gig and plays it out.

Concierge:
In the middle of the night? That's not OK.

Athena:
He needs to soundproof his place.

————————

Scene 2: Athena and her son are having dinner.
Someone knocks on the front door.

Upstairs Neighbor:
Hi, Umm. I'm Chris. I live above you.

Athena:
Hi. How can I help you?

Chris:
I came by to apologize for the noise last night. It won't
happen again.

Athena:
Nice to meet you, Chris. This is Garnet. He's a lot of fun at
2 in the morning. Garnet, say hi to our neighbor Chris. In
the future, Chris, if you wake him, he's yours.

Garnet:
(Waving, smiling.)

Chris:
Ha!

Athena:
I'm serious.

Chris:
Oh.

THE WORLD TURNED UPSIDE DOWN

Scene: Women bump into one another in a residential building lobby.

Dove:
Hey! Why are you here? Isn't today your day off?

Claudette:
(Nanny for a family in the building)

She begged me. He's away. Me thinks she scared of dem pickney dem. She can't be alone with them. Either he or I have to be there, or there had to be a play date or party. This year they're going away to camp for the whole summer.

Dove:
(Silence)

How's your son?

Claudette:
(Silence)

Fine. Wish I could spend more time with him.

BETTER YOU THAN WE

Scene: Parents hanging out in their car on the
four-day science trip drop-off carpool line,
waiting for the student buses to pull off. Jr. Teen's home
base teacher stops at our kid-free car to chat.

Parent:
Have fun.

(Giggle, giggle)

Teacher:
I love how parents say, "Have fun." Then follow it with a
demonic laugh. Muh ha ha.

IF THE SHOE FITS

Scene: Three teen male buddies sitting in a
sedan back seat discussing and dissing
sneakers.

Mavis:
You all should be wearing converse. Imma take you to a
Converse buy one get the second half off sale. That's all
you need, one high top, one low top.

All Boys:
(Laughter)

What?!

No way.

Not me.

I'd never rock those.

Nobody wears those.

Nobody cool.

Mavis:
Hey. I have Converse.

Sly:
Well. Umm. Those are great for moms.

Devon:
You can wear them.

Liam:
My mom has a pair. Thinks she's doing something when
she wears them. She gets all happy in them.

Mavis:

I love mine. They're cute. You kids don't know about shoes.

Devon:

Come to think of it; I've only seen them on moms.

Sly:

Actually, they are the perfect mom shoe—no need for moms to have Jordans or anything.

WHO CARES IF THEY SEE YOU SWEAT?

Scene: Mommy and the 23yo operate a day camp for three kids under ten years old.

9yo Girl:
Can we leave [the park]? I'm sweating.

Mommy:
That's natural. Means your body is working.

9yo Girl:
Not me. I don't sweat. Look, it's running down my back. Icky!

Mommy:
Of course, you do. Everyone sweats.

9yo Girl:
Nuh-uh. Not me. I don't sweat. I glisten. This is wrong.

Mommy:
That's just something people say to keep girls from having fun.

(Pointing to the other charges)

We're staying. Help them find lizards.

GIRLS TRIP

Scene: Women in a tropical hotel suite open-air living room

Savannah:
Alright, Ladies, we made it. We've managed a Girl's Trip despite evil forces and all-consuming responsibilities. I know, Corrine. We're women, not girls.

Corrine:
Yes. We are.

Savannah:
OK, women, we have almost a week to explore Santa Barbara. That's a lot of spa services, gourmet meals, and art.

Julie:
Don't forget concerts.

Corrine:
And wine!

Shante:
And men!

Julie:
Man. Singular. You're the only straight single woman here. We're married, and Corrine isn't into men. Or are you fluid these days, Darling?

Shante:
Men! It'll take more than one to handle all of this.

Corrine:
Hey! Corrine isn't shopping. That position has been filled.

Julie:
What?! You've been holding out. Spill it.

Savannah:
Hold on. Before we pick apart Corrine's love life, let's get organized.

Shante:
Boring!

Savannah:
We all have our roles. Shante brings the crazy. Corrine keeps us correct. Julie nurtures, and I organize.

Shante:
How 'bout you organize a pitcher of margaritas? We're thirsty.

Corrine:
I know that's right—time to eat, drink and be merry.

LEGACY

Scene: A group of professional women
bonding.

Kaia:
(Single Woman, No Kids)

It would have been nice to have kids. Someone to pass
on, share...

Gabby:
(Married Woman, 3 Kids)

Parenthood is mostly running all over town on your lunch
hour trying to find a sold-out Halloween costume.

All Mothers:
(Vigorous nodding)

Kaia:
Really?

Gabby:
Kids don't care about the rest. That's about you, not
them. Their priorities rule, and their priorities have nothing
to do with your accomplishments.

AGE AIN'T NOTHING BUT A NUMBER UNTIL YOU HEAR IT ALOUD

Scene: Tweens completing a survey regarding their experience and hopes for the after-school club I co-facilitated.

Preston:
Miss Brie. I think...

Brie:
Sweetheart, write it down. I'm too old to remember.

Preston:
How old are you?

Brie:
Older than you think.

Preston:
I think you're about 19.

Brie:
I can't be 19 if I have a son who is 23.

Preston:
Wow! Let's see...

-- Group discussion regarding NBA stars born to teenage mothers and coolness of me being able to become pregnant while in my mother's womb so that I could be 19 in 2016 --

Brie:

All of my children were born after I completed college and graduate school. I was an adult when they were born.

Wade:

According to my calculations, you are at least 56 years old.

Brie:

(In my head)

Have a seat, Wade.

ONCE GHOSTED, TWICE SHY

Scene: Reception in honor of the launch of
Paulina's new streaming show.

Celine:
Hey, girl. Long time no see. Proud of you. The show looks
great. How's the family?

Paulina:
Thanks for coming. I hope you're having a good time.
The team is working hard on the show. Glad you like it.

Celine:
I really do. Maybe we can do something together?

Paulina:
(Looking into the distance)

Maybe.

Celine:
That's it? I've been missing you, girl.

Paulina:
Thanks for coming out, Celine. I appreciate the support.

Celine:
Can we talk?

Paulina:
I'm a bit busy. Why don't you call next week, and we'll
set up something?

Celine:
Wow. It's like that?

Paulina:
Like what?

Celine:
You find a little success and forget those who knew you
when.

Paulina:
Excuse me. I didn't find success; I earned it. We could
have earned it together, but you ghosted me in the
middle of our joint project. Now you want to
collaborate? You dropped me. Remember?

Celine:
What? That was forever ago. Who even knows what
happened back then?

Paulina:
I do. I dropped everything to work with you on your
idea, and you stopped showing up. No communication,
nothing. Took a vacation with your man and stopped
returning my calls and texts. When you finally texted me
about something else, I asked what happened to our
project, and you deflected.

I wasted a lot of time wondering what I did to make you
treat me that way. Then thought maybe you were a
selfish user all along, and I'd missed it. That led me to
wonder how I could be such a poor judge of character.
Meanwhile, you still were MIA. Didn't hear from you
again until you were promoting your latest product.

Didn't invite me to your launch party or meetings. Just wanted me to get people to buy your stuff. For whatever reason, you saw our relationship as me serving you. Now that I have something you value, you want me back in your life.

Celine:
That's not how I remember it.

Paulina:
Hmm.

Celine:
I was busy, very busy doing other stuff. And my family needed me. I didn't have time for a vanity project with you. Now we can do it.

Paulina:
You could have told me that, maybe more politely. Vanishing wasn't cool. It wasn't a vanity project to me. We're all busy, but I made time for you. The project wasn't exactly what I wanted to work on at the time, but I was excited to work with you and see where it would lead us. Took me a while to recover from your ghosting. That's on me. I'm sensitive that way.

Celine:
I'm sorry you feel that way. We're good now. Right?

Paulina:
It's more than what I feel. It's what happened. But thanks for the apology.

I need to get back to the party. Pick up a goody bag on
your way out. There's fun stuff in there.

TALK IS CHEAP

Zach:
How can you do everything that you do? I'm impressed.

Mack:
I don't know. Other people do much more.

Zach:
No. Other people talk more about what they do.

GLASS HALF FULL

Scene: On the runway on a delayed plane
without air conditioning and water

Passenger 1:
(Grumbling about the flight troubles and the heat)

Passenger 2:
At least it's not Iraq.

Passenger 1:
(In a huffy know it all voice)

I don't know about that.

Passenger 2:

I do. It's not.

--Silence--

CODE SWITCHING

Gallia:
Notice you've become militant.

Sade:
Excuse me?

Gallia:
In school, you weren't so political, so racial.

Sade:
What does that mean?

Gallia:
I know we've been out of touch for years, and social media doesn't tell us all about someone, but your posts are always about race. The music you talk about isn't the same as what we listened to in school.

Sade:
Back then, I was in a permanent state of code-switching

Gallia:
What?

Sade:
I was behaving in a manner to fit in with the rest of you and allow you to feel comfortable with my Blackness by subduing it.

Gallia:
You were easier to hang out with. I wasn't scared of saying the wrong things or not knowing your references.

Sade:
You were more comfortable?

Gallia:
Yes.

Sade:
I wasn't. I'm more comfortable now, being my true self. Code-switching can be dishonest and exhausting.

Gallia:
What's wrong with blending in?

Sade:
Why should I? Why can't I be me, and you accept that? Or, if it's so important that we be similar, why don't you blend in with me?

Gallia:
That's impossible. I don't know the music and slang you use.

Sade:
You could learn them the same way I learned yours. Or, you could be, and I can be me. Back in school, I never asked you to be different for me to like you.

THE CRUSH

Felix:
We need to talk.

I don't want to be that guy, but I have to.

Emmett:
I get it. She has me all in.

Felix:
You can't help what you feel, but you're boarding on disrespecting what we're building. You can't turn off the feelings, but you need to distract yourself. Drown yourself in women. Keep searching until you find that feeling elsewhere. You don't have to stay away but maybe limit your alone time with me, woman. You feel me?

Emmett:
I hear you but

Felix:
No buts; I'm trying to save all the intermingling friendships—Ours, yours with her, and hers and mine. You've got to get distracted, or this'll be messy.

ABOUT THE AUTHOR

A sensitive thinker, who can sit still for days at a stretch, Kamyra Harding is an Atlanta-based wife, mother, daughter, friend, and mistake-maker. She's thrilled that her social media procrastination has yielded something other than an excuse to order takeout for dinner. This book is a compilation of conversations living in her mind. Some are true; others are imagined. Kamyra enjoys observing human interactions and words. What better way to combine the two than by eavesdropping on conversations? A simple conversation has the power to change a life. She exists on social media as the Try Hard Mommy. You can find her at http://www.TryHardMommy.com